What The Mistress Wants …
The Mistress Gets!

Part III

Grooming A Personal Slave

By

Mistress Vanessa

What The Mistress Wants …
The Mistress Gets!

Part III

Grooming A Personal Slave

By

Mistress Vanessa

real persons, places, or events is coincidental.

All Names have been changed in Activities, Narratives, and Events which are portrayed in this novel, as well as the Events which are described as taking place at any of the previous places where I was employed as a Dominatrix. All individuals involved in all activities, which are described in this book are over the age of twenty-one.

No one reading this Novel should ever undertake any of the actions described in this book without taking the appropriate safety precautions, as well as obtaining the mutual consent of their partner/partners, before engaging in such activity.

Table of Contents

A Good Day and A Good Night (From Part II)

After I had packed up my things and went out to the lobby to wait on Alicia and Joan, Kitty handed me $400 which was my share of the fee for Michael's session.

I smiled to myself as I tucked the money into my wallet next to the two Hundred Dollar bills which Michael had given to me as a tip. $600 for five hours work. Gosh I really do love my job!

Before he left, Michael said that the session had totally exceeded all his expectations, even though he was truly scared for a while when Comrade Yana had him convinced that she was going to turn him into a Eunuch.

Michael absolutely couldn't believe how well I was able to orchestrate such a complex session which incorporated every single one of his fantasies, even including the "big taboo fantasy" which he did not tell me about.

Michael couldn't thank me enough for everything that I had put into his session, and he assured me that I would definitely be the only Mistress that he would ever come to see.

I must admit that I was feeling very proud of myself at that moment having been able to pull off such an encompassing session. I was also happy that I had just added another slave to my rapidly growing stable.

When Alicia and Joan were finished, the three of us headed downstairs to Second Avenue to grab a cab.

As we stood on the sidewalk, Joan gave me a big hug, and said "Vanessa, you were truly a lifesaver for me today, helping me pull off my client's fantasy. I don't know how I can repay you for what you did for me".

With a very big smile I said, "Joan, right now my panties are dripping wet. I can't even begin to tell you how aroused and horny I am after the session that I had today. I know exactly how you can repay me when we get back to the apartment!"

Preparing for New Year's Eve

I really was glad that I had made the decision to stay in Manhattan during the holidays and not go home to New Jersey like I had done the prior year.

It was wonderful being able to experience the almost magical sights and sounds of New York at Christmas time. I was especially thrilled that Alicia and Joan had also decided to stay in the city over the holidays, as opposed to going home.

As a result of their decision, the three of us were able to go out to dinner and the theatre together, and really enjoy ourselves, not only out on the town, but also at home in the bedroom.

During December, Alicia, Joan and I were able to attend two Broadway plays. First, we went to see "Saturday Night Fever", and then a week later, we were fortunate enough to enjoy Lauren Bacall's performance in "Waiting In The Wings".

For me however, the highlight of the holiday season was the Christmas Spectacular at Radio City Music Hall starring the Rockettes. I absolutely loved the show and thought that the choreography was awesome.

The one time-honored New York activity which neither I nor Alicia and Joan even gave any serious consideration to participating in was going down to Times Square to watch the ball drop on

New Year's Eve, since we, like everyone else in New York had been constantly bombarded with non-stop gloom and doom predictions from every facet of the media about all of the terrible things which were going to happen when the clock struck midnight ushering in the new millennium know as Y2K.

Everyone had been told that once the year 2000 arrived, business and government computers would probably crash crippling our economy, that we could be without heat, electricity, and running water for long periods of time, and that we would not be able to get a penny out of our bank accounts, which were primarily controlled by computers, which wouldn't know how to deal with Y2K. Even Time Magazine released a foreboding special edition which insinuated that the end of the world would possibly arrive on January 1, 2000.

Instead of making plans to go down to Times Square on New Year's Eve, the three of us decided to have a Y2K party on December 31, 1999 and watch the big ball drop on television. We figured that if we had plenty to drink, got a little kinky, and everyone was in a party mood, we could deal with the chaos which might befall us all at 12:01 am on January 1, 2000

Alicia and Joan invited Kitty and her husband Jake, Jessica who was a friend of theirs and her husband Thomas, as well as Evelyn and Sarah who were Mistresses at our Dungeon, and everyone was excited about coming to the party. The week before our party, I decided to call my brother Rob to see what he was going to do on New Year's Eve.

He told me that he really hadn't made any plans and that he would probably wind up just taking his girlfriend Valerie out to dinner somewhere. He didn't sound all that enthusiastic about the idea.

When I mentioned the party which we were having at our apartment and inquired as to whether he would be interested in joining us, Rob immediately became excited, and said "Wow Sis, I would love to come up there to New York for your party on New Year's Eve. You can count on me being there!"

I was thrilled that Rob would be coming up for the party. I hadn't seen my brother since the beginning of the year, when he had his kinky little Ménage à trois with Alicia and Joan at our apartment. I told Rob that it was perfectly ok if he also wanted to bring Valerie to the party.

He laughed, and said "No Sis, I'll pass on that. I am afraid that Valerie is extremely vanilla and that she wouldn't blend in very well with you and your roommates".

Rob then told me that he would make a room reservation right away so that he wouldn't have to impose on Alicia, Joan, and me, and that he would find a hotel which was close to our apartment. I told him that would be fine, and that I was looking forward to seeing him at the end of the month.

I was quite surprised when Rob called me back two days later, and asked "Hey Sis, do you remember my good friend Rick from high school?"

Yes, I definitely remembered Rick, the good looking jock who had Varsity letters in quite a few high school sports, so I said to my brother "Yes Rob, how can I forget Rick. You were always telling me that he had a crush on me, even though I was only a Sophomore when he was a Senior at school".

Rob chuckled, and said "Yes, that was very true. Rick thought that you were one of the sexiest girls in high school, but he told me that there was no way that he would ever make a move on my younger sister until she turned eighteen and I gave him my permission. In reality though, I think that he was intimidated by you even though he is two years older than you".

I laughed, and said "So what is Rick doing these days?"

"Well, that's the reason I am calling you. After we graduated, while I was in the Army, Rick went to college in Philly as a business major. When we got together a few months ago in Jersey, he told me that he was working as a Stockbroker for a major brokerage house in Manhattan".

"Wow that's nice, a Stockbroker here in the city?"

"Yes, I don't really follow the market, but Rick said that the stock market has been hitting record highs all year, and that he has been doing quite well as a result of the bull market. Anyway, I called him to let him know that I was coming to Manhattan, and to see if he wanted to get together while I was in the city. He thought that was a great idea, and he told me to forget about reserving a hotel room. Rick told me that his feelings would be hurt if I didn't stay at his apartment in Tribeca, which is not too far from your place. He even said that he would take me to the Islanders vs Flyers game if I stayed an extra day".

Rob paused for a second, and then said "Sis, I was wondering if you would mind if I invited Rick to come with me to your New Year's Eve Party?"

"I would not mind at all Rob. I know that he has always been a good friend of yours and it will be interesting to see what he looks like after all these years". Then with a snicker, I said "It will also be quite interesting to see if your friend Rick still has a crush on me!"

With some hesitation, Rob said "I don't know about that, but I am sure that it will be priceless to see his reaction when he meets you and your roommates, especially if Joan and Alicia dress the way that they normally do. Maybe I better clue him in ahead of time as to what the three of you do for employment these days?"

I found my brother's comment to be somewhat hilarious and said, "Whatever you think is best Rob". Then to get in a little personal dig, I said "After all, you have had first hand experience dealing with my roommates, so you know best!"

New Year's Eve – December 31, 1999

While Alicia and I took care of cleaning the apartment and putting up the decorations, Joan went all out handling the arrangements for the food and liquor for our party.

She had made arrangements with our favorite Italian restaurant on Third Avenue to prepare and deliver the trays of food which she had ordered. Joan also had the liquor store down the block from our apartment deliver a case of beer, as well as assorted brands of red and white wine, Grey Goose Vodka, Jack Daniels, and Tanqueray Gin.

When the food and liquor arrived around 7 pm, Alicia and I were amazed at everything that Joan had ordered. As far as we knew, we were supposed to have eleven people counting us at the party. Looking at the trays of lasagna, manicotti, meatballs, sausage, salads, and desserts, as well as all the bottles of liquor and mixers which covered the kitchen counter, one would think that we were expecting twenty to thirty people to show up at the party.

Alicia and I smiled at each other, and she said "Well, I guess that we will be eating Italian well into January".

We had told everyone to arrive at 9 pm, so after the trays of food were set up on the food warmers, all the dishes, glassware, and silverware were arranged on the kitchen counters, and Alicia had arranged a nice mix of cd's on the stereo system, the three of us went into our bedrooms to get dressed for the party.

I had recently purchased a new short black leather dress, so I thought the party would present me with the perfect opportunity to show it off.

I chose a skimpy black low cut push up bra, black leather garter belt, black silk panties, sheer black stockings, black patent pumps with four inch heels, and a black leather choker with crystal rhinestones to complete my outfit.

When I looked at myself in the full length mirror after getting dressed, I loved the way that the plunging neckline of the dress showcased a good portion of my breasts and the way that the dress accentuated my figure. At the same time however, I could see that the hemline of the leather dress was much shorter than I had anticipated, and I realized that I would have to be cautious when bending over otherwise everyone would see the top of my stockings and garters.

After fixing my hair and putting the finishing touches on my make-up, I went back out to the kitchen and poured myself a glass of Zinfandel while I waited for Alicia and Joan to finish getting dressed.

When the door to their bedroom finally opened, Joan stuck her head out, and said "Surprise! What do you think Vanessa?" before she and Alicia stepped out into the hallway.

I almost choked on the wine I was drinking when I saw that the two of them were wearing matching long sleeve skin tight red latex catsuits, which had a boned corset incorporated right into the catsuit. They both were also wearing matching knee high black and red lace up boots which had heels that were at least five inches high.

When I had chosen my leather outfit for the party, my goal was to look sexy, alluring, and irresistible, and after looking at myself in the mirror, I was confident that I had achieved that goal.

Alicia and Joan's outfits however, while definitely sexy and provocative, screamed "Dominatrix" loud and clear. The first thought which popped into my mind when I saw them was "Rob obviously won't have a problem at all with the way that they are dressed since he is very familiar with Alicia and Joan, but what is his friend Rick going to say?" At that point, I sincerely hoped that Rob had taken the time to give Rick a little background info on Alicia, Joan, and me.

I quickly put all those thoughts out of my head, smiled at Alicia and Joan, and said "You both look absolutely stunning. It looks like those latex outfits were painted onto you. I can't even imagine how you got into something so tight. What made you two decide to wear the same outfit?"

They both laughed, and Joan said "You're right. It isn't easy getting into something this tight, but we did it with the help of a lot of lube".

With a big smile, Alicia said "When we went shopping the other day and saw these latex outfits, we thought that it would be fun for both of us to wear matching kinky outfits, since we were looking for something a little outrageous for our Y2K party".

I laughed, and said "Well, I would have to say that you succeeded at finding outrageous outfits for the party tonight. When I got dressed, I was worried that this leather dress might be a bit too titillating for a home party, but now I would say that my outfit is very mundane compared to what the two of you are wearing".

Joan shook her head, and said "Oh no. Vanessa, you don't need to worry at all about your outfit. You look incredibly sexy and sensuous. I am sure that the men won't be able to take their eyes off you for a minute tonight!"

Just as I was thanking Joan for the compliment, the front door buzzer sounded, and as soon as she heard Kitty's voice, Joan pressed the button on the intercom which released the lock on the front door so that Kitty and Jake could come up to the apartment.

As soon as Joan opened the door, and Kitty and Jake came into the apartment, Kitty gave each of us a hug and wished us a Happy New Years.

Then standing there in her little black dress, Kitty looked at Alicia and Joan's outfits, and said "My, my girls, are you two working tonight? I don't remember seeing your names on the schedule".

We all laughed at her comment, and then Alicia said "Well Kitty, you never know. The night is still young, and we might just run into someone who needs to be dominated between now and the new year!"

While Joan led Kitty and Jake into the kitchen where Jake grabbed a bottle of beer and Joan poured a glass of Chardonnay for Kitty, Alicia answered the door bell and then welcomed Evelyn and Sarah, two of the Mistresses who we worked with at the House of Female Domination.

As we all exchanged hugs, I was glad to see that Evelyn and Sarah had shown up wearing outfits which were much more conservative than what Alicia and Joan had chosen.

Sarah was wearing a red silk blouse, tight leather jeans, and red high heel pumps, while Evelyn looked very sexy dressed in a white blouse, short black leather skirt, black nylons, and black high heel pumps.

A few minutes later, Jessica who was a good friend of Joan's arrived with her husband Thomas in tow and following right behind them was my brother Rob and his friend Rick.

As my brother and his friend entered the apartment, I couldn't help thinking to myself how attractive Rick was. He was even better looking than I remembered him from our high school days. Not to exaggerate at all, but upon seeing him for the first time in seven years, the thoughts that ran through my mind were "Damm, he's drop-dead gorgeous with that sandy blonde hair and those radiant blue eyes. Wow, and my brother said that Rick is a stockbroker here in Manhattan. This could be interesting".

I gave Rob a big hug and told him how glad I was that he was able to make it to the party. Rob stood back, looked at me from head to toe, and then in his best Billy Crystal voice, said "Sis, you look marvelous".

Rob then said "Vanessa, you remember my friend Rick?"

As I extended my hand to Rick, I was quite impressed with his outfit which consisted of khaki slacks, a blue button down oxford, a checkered twill blazer, and what appeared to be very expensive Cordovan Italian loafers. With a big smile, I said "I sure do. So nice to see you again Rick after all these years. I remember when you used to come over to the house to see my brother. Thanks so much for putting Rob up at your apartment while he's here in town".

Rick said "It's no problem at all Vanessa. I was thrilled that Rob was able to come up to the city and spend some time with me. It will give us a chance to catch up on everything that has been happening in our lives and also go see a hockey game together".

Then with a warm smile, Rick said "I also totally agree with the comment which your brother just made about your appearance. Vanessa, you look absolutely incredible. I wish that I would have known sooner than you have been right here in Manhattan all this time. I would have looked you up right away".

I chuckled, and then with a devious smile, I said "Well Rick, maybe you'll get a chance to make up for lost time now that you know where I am!"

I then ushered Rob and Rick away from the front door, and said "Rob, you of course already know Alicia and Joan, but I'll take you and Rick around and introduce you to everyone who is here. Let's go into the kitchen first so that you both can get a drink before you meet everyone"

While Rob stood there mixing a Vodka and Cranberry Juice drink for himself, I refilled my glass of wine and then I watched as Rick assembled everything he needed to make himself a Jack Daniels Manhattan on the rocks.

After a few minutes, I spun around when I heard Joan say "Rob, where have you been hiding yourself, you bad boy?"

She and Alicia both walked over to my brother and gave him a big hug, and then Joan kissed Rob on his right cheek and Alicia kissed him on his left cheek, leaving imprints of their bright red lipstick on each of Rob's cheeks.

Then wagging her finger at my brother in a threatening manner, Joan said "Rob, why have you been neglecting us all year? Why haven't you come up to see us, especially after all the fun we had playing with you the last time you visited?"

It was very obvious that Rob was completely embarrassed by Joan's comment, since Rick and I were standing there and heard what Joan said. After a long pause, Rob meekly said, "I am so sorry Joan, but I've been very busy at work and I haven't had a chance to break away and get up here to New York".

At that point Alicia chimed in and said, "Well, I don't buy that excuse at all Rob. We'll just have to make time to punish you while you are here since you've been neglecting us for so long".

Rob's face was bright red, and he looked like he just wanted to crawl under the table. I was laughing to myself about his predicament when I realized that neither Rob or I had introduced Rick to Alicia and Joan.

When I turned to Rick, I immediately noticed from the expression on his face and the way he was looking intently at Joan and Alicia, that he was totally enthralled by the two latex clad goddesses standing in front of him. I could see that his eyes kept wandering up and down from the stiletto heels on their boots up to the top of their corsets.

I coughed a few times to get his attention and to break him out of his trance, and said "Rick, I'd like you to meet my roommates Alicia and Joan".

As soon as he had regained his composure, Rick shook each of their hands, and said "It is truly my honor and pleasure to meet both of you. Thank you both so much for allowing me to attend your party".

Alicia smiled, and said "Nice to meet you also Rick. We are glad that you were able to come. However, you should be thanking Vanessa not us since she is the one who invited you to the party".

As she and Joan turned and started to walk out of the kitchen, Alicia turned back to Rick, and in true Alicia style said, "Now Rick, you make sure that you take care of Vanessa because if I should hear that you do anything to upset her or displease her, I will just have to get my whip out and do something about it, and I can assure you that you will not like it if I have to get my whip out!"

I couldn't believe (then again … yes, I could, knowing Alicia) that she actually said that to someone who she just met. Rick stood there with his mouth hanging open, not knowing what to say, but it was obvious to me, judging from the tent protruding at the crotch area of his khaki pants, that Alicia's outfit and what she had just said to him had gotten him very excited.

Over the next half hour, I took charge of Rob and Rick and introduced them to everyone at the party, including the couple who were friends of Joan who I had not met before. When we got to Jessica and Thomas, I introduced myself first, and then my brother and Rick.

After Rob and Rick had met everyone, we returned to the kitchen to freshen up our drinks. A few minutes later while Rob was engaged in a conversation with Sarah and Evelyn, I turned to Rick, and feeling somewhat emboldened by the three glasses of wine which I had already consumed, I asked him if he would like a personal tour of the rest of the apartment. When he said yes, I led him down the hall and showed him first the enormous bathroom and then I took him into Alicia and Joan's room.

I smiled to myself as soon as I witnessed the somewhat shocked expression on Rick's face as he stood there and studied the massive wooden bed with all the bondage rings, the FemDom artwork on the walls, and the assortment of bondage paraphernalia which Alicia and Joan had left lying around their room.

I wanted to gauge his reaction to what he saw, so I said, "Well Rick, what do you think of my roommates' bedroom?"

He hesitated for a moment, and then said "I would have to say that it is very interesting, and I haven't seen a bedroom like this before. I can see now that Rob wasn't pulling my leg when he said that your roommates were into some heavy kinky stuff".

I laughed, and said "No Rick, my brother wasn't pulling your leg. Come on, I'll show you my bedroom".

Rick followed me down the hall into my bedroom, and after he looked all around, he said "Well, this is more like the bedrooms which I am used to".

I laughed and said "Don't let appearances fool you Rick. Maybe, I just keep my kinky toys hidden better than my roommates".

I could tell that my remark caught Rick completely off guard, but after a moment of silence, he said "Vanessa, was Rob serious when he told me that you are also working as a Dominatrix like your roommates?"

I smiled and said "Yes Rick, my brother was totally serious. I work at The House of Female Domination just like Alicia and Joan".

Whether I was motivated by all the alcohol which I had consumed, or by the pure animal magnetism generated by a truly attractive male, I subtly reached over and closed the door to my bedroom. Then pressing my leather clad body up against Rick and forcing his back up against the wall, I asked "So tell me Rick, what was your reaction when my brother told you that I was working here in the city as a Dominatrix?"

Rick hesitated answering me, and it was very obvious to me that he was giving serious consideration to what would be the proper response to my question. Finally, he said "I have to be completely honest with you Vanessa. Ever since Rob told me what you have been doing, I've had constant erotic thoughts about you dressed in leather and dominating men while they are on their knees. Then coming here tonight and seeing you dressed as you are in that sexy leather dress and heels has kept me excited and aroused since I walked through the door. All I've thought about so far tonight is how exciting it would be to have you dominate me".

I looked Rick directly in the eyes, and asked "Have you ever been dominated by a woman?"

Rick lowered his head a little to avoid looking into my eyes and said "Just once, and that was by a professional Dominatrix. Vanessa, I've known for years that contrary to what people think about me, I really am not a confident alpha male when it comes to dealing with women. My idea of a perfect relationship would be one where I was submissive to a dominate female. Unfortunately, I have never been lucky enough to date a dominant woman who was willing to take control of our relationship. So, when I first moved here to Manhattan and saw all the newspaper ads for Dommes, I thought that I would take a chance and go visit one".

"Yes, and how did you like it?"

"I truly enjoyed surrendering all control, being put into different types of bondage, being disciplined, and being forced to worship the Mistress's boots as a sign of my submission. The whole experience got me very sexually aroused".

"So, if you liked it so much, how come you only went once to see a Domme since you've lived here?"

"Because it didn't really address my problem. Even though I thoroughly enjoyed the experience with the professional Domme, I found it to unfulfilling the next day, when I realized that it was a one shot thing, and that I still had not succeeded in finding a true dominant woman with whom I could share a real lasting and loving relationship".

Looking back now, I realize that it was a little premature on my part and I really put Rick on the spot, but at the time it seemed like the perfect question to ask him, so I lifted his face up so that he had to look directly into my eyes, and I said "So Rick, do you think that I am the kind of dominant woman with whom you would like to have a lasting and loving relationship?"

He didn't hesitate for a second, and quickly said "Oh, without a doubt Vanessa. I would love to serve someone like you!"

I smiled, reached down and placed my hand on Rick's crotch where his cock was visibly pressing against the fabric of his pants, and said "Well, I am glad to hear that. Rob told me many times that you always had a crush on me. Was his assessment correct?"

"Oh God yes Vanessa. I always thought that unlike most of the other flaky women who tried to get my attention, you were always much more mature and in control. And whenever I would come over to your house to see your brother, I had to really control my emotions. I've always thought that you were the most attractive and sexiest female who I ever met".

I am considered tall at five foot seven inches, and normally Rick would be about three inches taller than me. However, as I stood there in my four inch heels, pressing my body against him, I actually was in a position to bring my lips down to his, and while I tempted him with the possibility of a kiss, I asked "So Rick, putting aside the fact that I am a Dominatrix, do you still think that I am the most attractive and sexiest female who you have ever met?"

Without hesitating for a second, Rick said "Absolutely Vanessa. There's no doubt in my mind. As soon as I saw you tonight, I realized that you are even sexier and much more beautiful than I remembered".

I smiled at Rick, and then I pressed my lips against his, and gave him a long passionate kiss, before slipping my tongue into his mouth, while he wrapped his arms around my waist and pulled me up against his body even tighter. Our lips stayed locked together for the longest time while our tongues explored each other's mouth.

Just when I thought that our kiss would never end, there was a knock on my bedroom door, and Joan said "Vanessa, sorry to interrupt whatever you are doing in there, but we started serving dinner. I thought I'd let you know that everyone is eating now".

I broke away from Rick's embrace, opened the door, smiled at her, and said "Thanks Joan, we'll be right there".

I gave Rick a quick kiss on the cheek and said, "Let's go get something to eat. We'll finish our discussion later tonight and I'll see if you really are ready to submit to me".

Then before walking out into the hallway, I laughed, and patted Rick's crotch, and said "You better think about something else real fast and lose that hard-on before you go out into the kitchen!"

The Ball Drops & The World Doesn't End on January 1, 2000

Everyone loved the food which Joan had ordered for the party. Even after quite a few people had a second serving there still was a tremendous amount of food left over, and I realized that Alicia was right when she said that we would be eating Italian well into the month of January.

After everyone had their coffee and dessert, and sat around the living room talking, Alicia passed out noise makers which she had bought especially for the party. She then shut the stereo off and turned on the television so that we could watch the festivities from Times Square. We were surprised to see that because of the new millennium which would be arriving in a few minutes, Dick Clark and Peter Jennings were doing a special show for Y2K called "ABC 2000" instead of the normal Rockin' New Year's Eve Special.

As soon as the clock struck midnight and the big ball dropped, everyone started kissing, rattling their noise makers, and wishing each other a Happy New Year. After I had hugged my brother and everyone else at the party, I embraced Rick and gave him a long sensuous kiss.

When our lips finally parted, Rick said "Wow, after that I need to go make myself another drink. Would you like me to refill your wine for you?"

I handed him my glass, and said "Yes, that would be very nice".

I then turned to Joan and Alicia and said "Well, it's January 1, 2000 and the lights are still on, and it doesn't look like the world has ended".

They laughed, and Joan said "Well I for one, am glad that all those predictions were wrong. Alicia and I have something in mind for that brother of yours after all the other guests leave, and I would have been quite pissed if the world would have ended and messed up our plans!"

When I heard that, I said "Oh no. What are you two up to now? It's sounds like Rob might be in trouble. Maybe I better warn my dear brother".

Alicia shook her head and said, "Vanessa, don't you even think about saying anything to him and messing up our plans. You just mind your own business".

Then with a big smile, Joan pointed towards the kitchen where Rick was making a drink and said, "I would bet that you also have something planned for that handsome hunk of a man after everyone leaves, and that you probably won't be too concerned about what we do to your brother".

I laughed, and said "Yes, I suppose that you are right about that".

During the next hour all the guests started to depart, until finally around 2 am, only Rob and Rick were still there with me, Alicia, and Joan.

As the five of us sat in the living room, sipping our drinks and talking, Joan had many questions for Rick about the stock market and where he thought she should be investing her money.

When I asked Rob if he had drove his car over to our apartment, he told me that he had left it in the parking garage next to Rick's apartment, and that the two of them had taken a cab to our party.

"Smart move Rob. You don't need to be driving in this city tonight with all the drunks out there on the road".

About fifteen minutes later, Alicia excused herself and went into her bedroom. Not even five minutes later, Joan stood up, turned to my brother and said "Rob, could I borrow you for a minute. I need some help taking care of something in my bedroom".

Rob quickly jumped up to his feet, said "Sure, no problem", and he followed Joan as she led him into her bedroom.

I smiled to myself because I knew that my dear brother was about to become the prey for my two roommates, and that I probably would not be seeing him again till sometime later in the day.

As soon as Rob and Joan had disappeared into her bedroom, I stood up, pointed my finger at Rick, and motioned for him to follow me into my bedroom.

He didn't hesitate for a second. Rick dutifully sprung up from the couch and followed behind me as I headed down the hall to my bedroom.

As soon as Rick and I entered the bedroom, I locked the door behind us. I then went over to the armoire in the corner, opened it, and took out a black gym bag which contained all of my special toys, and I placed the bag next to the high back chair which was located on the other side of my room.

I moved the ottoman out of the way, sat down in the chair, crossed my long legs, and said to Rick "I would like you to get completely naked now. Then we can finish the discussion which we started earlier if you are still interested in serving me".

Rick hesitated for a moment, but when I stared him down, he realized that he had no choice other than to do what I had told him to do. He slowly began to get undressed. When he had removed all of his clothes except his briefs, he stood there in front of me with his cock pushing out against the front of his tight briefs.

I looked at him, and said "Rick, did you not understand what I said? I said completely naked!"

At that point he slipped his fingers into the waistband of his briefs, pushed them down his legs, and stepped out of them. As soon as he removed his briefs, his penis sprung up hard and erect out in front of him, and I must say that I was quite impressed with the length and girth of his cock.

I intentionally changed the intonation of my voice over to a more dominant pitch and said "Come here Rick. Stand in front of me!"

As soon as he moved over in front of my chair, I grabbed his swollen cock, pulled him towards me, and said "It looks to me like someone is very excited, and we haven't even started our discussion yet.

I reached down into my gym bag, took out a condom and handed it to Rick, and said "Put this on right now. I am afraid that you might not be able to control yourself, and I am not about to let you drip all over my beautiful carpet".

After Rick had opened the package, and slipped the rubber down over his hard cock, I said "Yes, that's much better. You can get down on your knees in front of me now!"

As Rick knelt in front of me, I swung my foot back and forth, and noticed that his eyes were intently focused on the stiletto heel which was swinging in front of his face.

"Ok Rick, I am going to ask you some questions and I want you to give serious thought to my questions before you answer me. Do you understand?"

He quickly nodded his head and said, "Yes Vanessa. I understand".

"Good. Rick, are you completely sure that you want to totally submit to me? If we should embark on a relationship, are you really ready to surrender all control to me? Do you understand that if I decide to have a relationship with you, I will be in control at all times, and I will expect you to do anything and everything which I tell you to do without question? Rick, I may take you as my lover, but you will also be my slave. Do you fully understand what I am saying to you?"

After a few seconds, Rick nodded his head, and said "Yes Vanessa. I fully understand what you are saying to me, and yes, I am ready to submit to you. I have had the desire for the longest time to have a relationship where I could submit to a dominant woman and turn over total control to her. I am absolutely thrilled that I might have the opportunity to serve you, because I have never met another woman who is as beautiful and dominant as you. Yes, I am definitely ready to turn over control of my life to you if you will have me".

I smiled and said "So be it then Rick. From this minute forward, you will always address me as Mistress Vanessa when we are together, and I will expect you to be totally subservient to all my wishes. I will be your Mistress and you will be my slave. Do you understand what I am saying?"

Rick immediately nodded his head and said "Yes, Mistress Vanessa".

"Very Good slave. When we are together in the company of other people, you may call me Vanessa unless I tell you otherwise. Do you understand slave?"

"Yes Mistress".

I smiled at how fast Rick had adapted to properly addressing me as his Mistress. I then reached into the bag next to my chair and took out a pair of handcuffs.

"Turn around slave and place your hands behind your back!"

As soon as Rick did what I said, I locked the handcuffs around his wrists, restraining his arms behind his back. I then pushed his head down to the top of my pumps and said, "Slave, you can show me how much you want to serve me by diligently cleaning my shoes with your mouth and tongue!"

Without saying a word, Rick immediately brought his mouth down to my left pump and began licking and kissing it. He worked his tongue all over the top and sides of my pump until it glistened from his adoration.

At that point, I raised my shoe up off the ground, and ordered Rick to lick the sole of my shoe clean and to suck on my stiletto heel.

I was happy to see that he quickly followed my order without any argument. After he had licked every inch of the sole, I slipped the four inch heel into his mouth, and made him suck on it until it was totally clean.

I then crossed my legs, and placed my right shoe down onto the floor, and told Rick that I expected him to show the same worship to that shoe which he had shown to my other high heel pump.

After Rick had thoroughly cleaned the top and sides of my right shoe with his mouth and tongue, I then lifted it up off the floor and I was glad to see that without me saying a word to him, Rick quickly began licking the sole of my right shoe and sucking on the stiletto heel.

When I was satisfied with the job that Rick had done cleaning my pumps, I stood up, unlocked the handcuff on his right wrist, and ordered him to place his arms out in front of him. I then relocked the handcuff around his right wrist, restraining his arms in front of him.

Just then I heard what sounded like someone in the kitchen, and I assumed that it was either Joan or Alicia, so I reached over to the table, picked up my almost empty wine glass, handed it to Rick, and told him to go out to the kitchen and get me a fresh glass of wine. I figured that I would subject him to a little humiliation so that he would get used to it.

He hesitated just a little too long for my liking, obviously dubious about going out to the kitchen naked with his wrists handcuffed in front of him, so I reached down into my bag, retrieved a riding crop, and brought it down very hard twice across Rick's ass, and said "Why are you still standing there, slave? Did you not understand what I just told you to do?"

Rick apologized to me and scurried out of the bedroom, headed to the kitchen to refill my wine glass. While Rick was in the kitchen, I took some items which I planned on using on him out of my bag and placed them on the nightstand next to the bed.

A few minutes later when Rick returned to the bedroom with my glass of wine, I saw that his face was beet red, and with a big smile on her face, Alicia walked in right on his heels, and said "Vanessa, I went out to the kitchen to refill the wine glasses for Joan and me and this nicely endowed stud of yours walked in sporting an impressive hard-on. I can see that you are going to have a lot of fun with him. When you're done with him, feel free to send him into our bedroom. I am sure that Joan and I can put him to good use after we are done using your brother!"

I laughed, and said "Thanks for the offer Alicia, but I plan on keeping this slave right here and using him for my pleasure all night. You and Joan have fun with my brother!"

As soon as Alicia left my bedroom, I took the glass of wine from Rick, and ordered him up onto the bed on his back. Once he was lying on the bed, I took a short length of chain and a padlock out of my bag and secured his handcuffs to the brass headboard of my bed, restraining his arms up above his head.

I then locked a set of leather cuffs onto Rick's ankles, and using a sturdy piece of rope, tied the ankle cuffs down taut to the brass footboard of my bed.

"Are you starting to feel helpless slave?"

Rick nodded his head and said, "Yes Mistress".

"Good slave!"

I then sat on the edge of the bed, ran the tip of my riding crop over Rick's nipples, getting him totally aroused, and said "Now slave, since you and I have never been together before, I don't know what your pain threshold is, or what your hard limits are at this point. Therefore, I need you to select a safe word. Do you know what a safe word is?"

"Yes Mistress. I've read a lot of Female Domination magazines and have visited quite a few of the BDSM websites. I know what you are referring to".

"Good slave, so what safe word would you like to use for our new relationship?"

Rick thought about my question for a minute, and then said, "Bull Market".

I laughed and said "Well, that's more than one word, but I suppose that I can allow you to use that slave".

Then as I ran my riding crop up and down the length of Rick's rock hard cock, I said "Slave, you need to understand that if I am torturing you or punishing you, and you absolutely can not tolerate what I am doing, then you need to use your safe word. I will not stop what I am doing to you under any circumstances unless you utter your safe word. Do you understand what I am telling you?"

Rick nodded his head and said "Yes Mistress Vanessa. I understand".

"Very Good slave"

I then stood up and removed my leather dress and walked over to the closet and I hung it up. When I walked back over to the bed, I could see that Rick's hard cock was now bouncing up and down, obviously stimulated by the fact that I was standing over him in my lingerie and heels.

I bent down, and began sucking and gently biting Rick's nipples, getting him totally aroused. As soon as he began moaning from the pleasure which I was giving him, I reached over to the nightstand, picked up a pair of cloverleaf nipple clamps, and snapped the clamps down over his erect nipples.

Rick immediately cried out because of the pain which the clamps inflicted on his nipples. I lowered my face down to his, gave him a long passionate kiss, and then said "Now slave, we're just getting started. I haven't really given you any pain at all. You need to be quiet and not disturb my roommates or else I will be forced to gag you. Do you understand?"

Still grimacing from the pain of the nipple clamps, Rick nodded his head and said, "Yes Mistress".

I didn't let Rick know what I was feeling at that moment, but after many months of not having sexual relations with a man, I was totally aroused by his helplessness and the sight of his prodigious cock bouncing up and down in front of me. I could tell that my thong was completely soaked from the moisture which I felt between my legs.

I was very thankful and had truly enjoyed all of the orgasms which I had received over the past year from both Joan and Alicia's tongues, but as I stood there looking down at Rick bound helplessly to my bed, I realized that there was nothing that I wanted more at that point than to feel that big cock of his in my pussy. I also knew that I could use him any way I wanted for my pleasure and there was nothing he could do to stop me.

I reached down and pulled up on the chain which was connected to the clamps on Rick's nipples, and he immediately let out a loud cry of anguish.

I shook my head and told him that the noise he was making was unacceptable, and that I had already warned him once that he needed to be quiet, so now I would have to gag him.

I slipped my panties which were already dripping wet from my sexual arousal, down my legs, bent over Rick, and shoved the panties into his mouth, and said "Here slave my panties will help keep you quiet and you can also suck all my precious juices out of them".

I then climbed up onto the bed, straddled Rick's legs, and pulled the condom off of his cock, and threw it onto the floor. After having gone so many months without sexual intercourse, there was no way that I wanted to feel a rubber. I wanted to feel every inch of Rick's hard cock which was standing up erect in front of me.

As I moved my body up over his crotch, Rick tried to raise his groin up so that his cock could meet my pussy. I quickly picked up the riding crop which was lying on the bed next to me and brought it down hard over first his right nipple and then his left nipple.

Rick let out a bloodcurdling scream which was muffled somewhat by my panties which were balled up in his mouth.

I then admonished him saying "Slave, you try that again, and I will give you a whipping you won't forget for a long time. I am the one who is in control here and I plan on using you primarily for my pleasure, so don't even move a muscle unless I give you permission. Do you understand?"

With a look of fear on his face, Rick nodded his head and mumbled that he understood me.

I then positioned my pussy over the tip of his cock, and slowly began lowering myself down onto his long and thick shaft. As I pressed my pussy further down over Rick's wide cock, I could feel a sexual arousal sweep over my entire body like nothing that I had experienced in many months.

When the entire length of Rick's sizable cock was engulfed in my pussy, I began rocking my body back and forth, stimulating my vulva and sending pleasurable waves throughout my body. As soon as Rick started moaning from the stimulation which his cock was receiving, I immediately pulled on the chain attached to his nipple clamps, and said "Slave, don't you even think about coming until I give you permission. You will come exactly when I tell you to come!"

With Rick's cock fully impaling me, I moved my pussy back and forth faster and faster until I felt the waves of an impending orgasm rushing over me. I dug my stiletto heels deep into the sides of Rick's thighs, pushed my pussy down even tighter against his crotch, squeezed both of my breasts, and loudly cried out as I enjoyed an explosive orgasm unlike any I had experienced in a quite a long time. As the orgasm swept over me, I yanked on the chain, pulling the clamps off of Rick's nipples and said "Come now slave. I want you to come now and fill my pussy up with your cum!"

I didn't have to tell him a second time. Before I even started coming back down to earth after my incredible orgasm, I immediately felt Rick's cock pulsating and forcibly shooting stream after stream of cum into my pussy.

When I had totally regained my composure and realized that Rick's cock was totally spent, I raised my pussy up, slid onto his stomach, and pulled my wet panties out of his mouth.

I then brought my mouth down to his, gave him a long hot kiss, and when our lips parted, I said "Thank you slave. That was exactly what I needed, and how are you doing?"

Rick looked up at me, smiled and said "I am just wonderful Mistress. That was incredible. Thank you so very much!"

"You are quite welcomed slave. I am glad that you enjoyed that as much as I did".

Then with a devious smile on my face, I said "There is one more thing however that you need to take care of slave before I release you".

With a quizzical look on his face, Rick asked "What is that Mistress?"

Instead of answering him, I just slid my body up onto his face, pressed my pussy down over his mouth and said "You need to clean up that mess you just made in my pussy slave. Make sure that you lick me totally clean!"

Restrained helplessly to the bed as he was, and with me sitting on his face, Rick had no option other than to do what I had just told him to do.

He slipped his tongue into my pussy and began licking me and sucking out the what was the combination of his cum and my vaginal juices.

As Rick licked and sucked my pussy clean, I soon felt myself becoming totally aroused once again, and said "You are doing a great job slave licking my pussy clean. I want you to also suck on my clit and give me some more pleasure now!"

Rick quickly followed my command and began sucking on my clit while his tongue continued to dart in and out of my pussy. Within minutes, I could feel myself once again on the edge of experiencing another orgasm.

I began pressing my pussy down tighter against Rick's face, and as he was obviously struggling to breathe, he became more excited, and sucked on my clit faster and faster while his tongue shot in and out of my pussy like crazy.

Within moments, I felt another wonderful orgasm sweep over my body, and as it advanced from my toes up to my head, I screamed out "Oh yes slave. Don't stop slave!"

When I finally stopped shaking and recovered from having experienced the second wonderful orgasm of the night (or rather I should say early morning), I slid down off of Rick's face, and retrieved the key to the handcuffs out of the nightstand next to the bed. I unlocked the handcuffs, freeing Ricks wrists, and then laid down next to him on the bed and said "That was absolutely wonderful. I think that you might just work out fine as my personal slave!"

A New Year and A New Relationship

The last thing which I remembered after my love making session with Rick was looking at the clock on the nightstand next to the bed and noticing that it was 4 am before I laid my head down onto Rick's chest and cuddled with him as he held me tight. I was so emotionally and physically drained from the wonderful orgasms which I had enjoyed from Rick's cock and mouth, and from the effect of all of the wine which I had consumed, that as I laid there with him in the wee hours of the morning, I immediately passed out and fell soundly asleep.

When I finally woke up and opened my eyes, I thought for a moment that maybe my wonderful sexual escapade had only been a dream, but I quickly realized that no, it wasn't a dream when Rick gave me a hug and said, "Good Morning Mistress".

I lifted my head up, gave him a long passionate kiss, and then said, "Good Morning slave".

When I looked over at the clock on the nightstand and saw that it was almost noon, I bolted up from the bed, and said "Wow slave, you really wore me out. I've never slept this late".

Rick laughed and said "I beg to differ with you Mistress, but if you recall I was in no position to do anything last night. You were the one calling all the shots".

I smiled, leaned over the bed and gave him another long kiss, and said "Yes, I suppose that you are right, and it was all wonderful!"

Then Rick lowered his voice, and meekly said "Mistress, I really have to go to the bathroom. I've been awake, and I've been holding it for quite some time. I was going to go to the bathroom and also take a shower, but I did not want to wake you up since you were sleeping so peacefully".

I pointed to the door and said "That was very nice slave that you waited to ask permission to use the bathroom. Go ahead and take care of your business".

Rick pointed down to his ankles which were still restrained to the footboard of the bed, and said "Well, I would love to, but I am not really in a position to go anywhere".

When I realized that I had released his wrists after our lovemaking, but had neglected to release his ankles, I started laughing, and then jokingly said "Oh my goodness. I might just leave you like that for the rest of the day so that you'll be ready and accessible in case I need to use that mouth or cock of yours again!"

I then grabbed a key out of the nightstand and unlocked the little padlocks which were on the leather ankle cuffs and freed Rick so that he could get up off the bed. After he jumped into his underwear and his slacks, Rick made a beeline to the bathroom to relieve himself and take a shower.

I then realized that after our lovemaking, I had fallen asleep without removing my bra, garter belt, stockings or high heel pumps, so rather than getting undressed, I just threw a silk robe on over my lingerie and headed to the kitchen to get a cup of coffee.

When I walked into the kitchen, I saw that Rob was sitting in the living room, drinking a cup of coffee and watching the Rose Bowl Parade with the volume turned down very low on the television so that he wouldn't disturb anyone.

As I poured myself a cup of coffee, I said "Good Morning or I suppose that I should say Good Afternoon Rob. Have you been up very long?"

"Yes sis, actually I have been up for almost three hours now. I've already had a shower, and I am on my third cup of coffee".

I grabbed my cup of coffee, went into the living room, and sat down on the couch opposite Rob, and said "I am surprised that you were up so early, especially since nobody got to bed at a decent hour".

Rob smiled, and said "Well, I didn't get much sleep anyway as it was. Sometime after 5 am when Alicia and Joan were done using me for their pleasure, they left me hogtied on the floor by their bed. Damn, they tied me up so tight, that no matter how hard I tried, I couldn't get free. When Joan got up and untied me this earlier this morning, I quickly jumped under the hot water in the shower so that I could work the kinks out of my body".

I started laughing uncontrollably and said "My dear brother. See, now you know what can happen when you play with big girls like Alicia and Joan!"

Rob nodded his head, and said "Boy sis, isn't that the truth.

Then with a big smile, I said "I hope that my roommates at least allowed you to have some relief since they obviously got all the pleasure from you that they wanted".

I could see that Rob was somewhat embarrassed by my comment, but he sheepishly said, "Yes sis, I have no complaints in that area".

Just then Alicia and Joan, who were already dressed and ready for the day. walked into the living room, went over to Rob, and both of them gave him a kiss. Then Joan turned to me and said, "Did we just hear someone mention our names?"

I smiled, and said "Yes, you did. My dear brother was just telling me about the compromising position which you put him into when you were done playing with him this morning".

Rob's face turned bright red, and Joan laughed, and said "Yes, that was somewhat mean of Alicia and I, especially after Rob serviced both of us so well with the talented mouth and tongue of his, but we did warn him earlier that he would be punished for neglecting us for so many months. I am sure that he will be paying us a visit on a much more frequent basis from now on!"

As soon as I got up to refill my coffee cup, Rick completely dressed and looking like he was ready to pose for the front cover of GQ walked into the kitchen, came over to me, and gave me a kiss. Then he whispered in my ear "Thank you so very much Mistress Vanessa".

I smiled, grabbed another cup, filled it with coffee, handed it to Rick, and whispered into his ear "You are quite welcomed. Just remember that today is the first day of your new life as my personal slave!"

Alicia pointed at us in the kitchen, and said "What are you two whispering about in there?"

Then she snickered and said "Vanessa, you sure weren't whispering early this morning. You were moaning so loud that we were able to hear your cries of passion even in our room!"

I stuck my tongue out at her and said, "Alicia, it sounds like maybe you're jealous that I didn't send Rick down to your room like you asked!"

Then I picked up my coffee cup, headed towards my bedroom, and said "Since I'm the only one who isn't dressed yet, I think I better go get my shower now".

After my shower, I put on a pair of low cut jeans, a red halter top, and a pair of red high heels. When I returned to the living room, Joan got up, shut the television off, and said "We've been waiting for you Vanessa. We decided that we would all go up to the Second Avenue Deli and have Brunch. How does that sound to you?"

"That sounds wonderful. I know that it's hard to believe but I am starving right now even though I ate all that wonderful food last night".

Alicia, never being one to miss a chance to take a shot at someone, turned to Rick, and said "Sounds to me like you helped her work off all that lasagna which she ate last night!"

The meal at the Second Avenue Deli was great as usual. The five of us had a wonderful lunch, laughing and sharing stories for almost two hours while we ate. Even after having had their pastrami many times, I still found myself being amazed at how huge and delicious their sandwiches always were.

After we were finished eating and everyone was getting ready to leave the Deli, I took Rick aside where no one could hear us, and I handed him one of my business cards on which I had also written my home phone number. As soon as he also handed me one of his business cards with all of his phone numbers, I said "Ok slave, I will assume that you were very serious last night when you said that you were ready to serve me without question. So, from this point forward when I call you, I will expect you to do whatever I say and to do it promptly!"

Rick immediately nodded his head and said "Yes Mistress. Absolutely".

I then reached into my purse, took out the black panties which I had worn the night before, the same panties which I had used to gag Rick. I handed them to him and said, "You keep these and smell my scent on them every day so that you are always reminded that you now belong to me, and that I alone control you!"

As soon as he shoved my panties into the side pocket of his sports coat, I brought my lips up to Rick's and gave him a long sensuous kiss. When I finally pulled my lips away from his, I said "Slave, don't doubt me at all when I tell you that from this point forward I plan on fully using you for my pleasure, service, and entertainment!"

Before Rick and Rob got into the cab which they had just hailed to head back to Rick's apartment in Tribeca, I gave my brother a big hug and said "Rob, now you enjoy the next few days with Rick, and don't you be a stranger this coming year. Whenever you get a chance, come up and see me".

Then with a devious smile, I said "I am sure that I don't need to tell you that if you want to stay on the good side of Alicia and Joan, you'll have to plan on making regular trips up here to the city to see them anyway".

Building My Clientele & Grooming My Personal Slave

On the Tuesday morning following New Year's Day, I returned to work at The House of Female Domination after having enjoyed eleven straight days off for the holidays. Kitty greeted me as soon as I walked into the lobby, and I thanked her once again for having given me the time off so that I was able to really experience the Christmas season in New York.

"It was no problem at all Vanessa. Actually, it was quite slow around here while you were off".

Then Kitty laughed and said "Not too many clients came in for a session during the week between Christmas and New Year's Day. They were all probably at home with their wives or girlfriends".

Then with a big smile, she asked "So how did you meet that gorgeous hunk that you were with at the party? Was it just my imagination, or did I detect that some serious sparks were flying between the two of you?"

I laughed, and said "No Kitty, it wasn't just your imagination. I've known Rick for many years, we just had not seen each other in almost seven years until the party the other night. It may be quite premature on my part, but I think that Rick is a keeper and I've decided to train him to be my personal slave!"

Slightly astonished, Kitty said "Wow. Good for you girl. Every woman should have their own personal slave!"

I then explained to Kitty how Rick who has been a close friend of my brother for many years, had gone to the same high school as I did and how he always had a crush on me, even though he never acted on it. I told her how he had moved to Manhattan after college to take a job as a Stockbroker down in the Financial District, and that he had absolutely no idea that I was also in New York until my brother invited him to the New Year's Eve party at my apartment.

"Gosh Vanessa. After not seeing him for so many years, it sounds like you two didn't waste any time at all jump-starting a relationship".

I laughed, and said "Yes, you are quite right about that, but as soon as I found out the other night that Rick had a submissive streak and a desire to serve a dominant woman, I decided to take advantage of it for my benefit".

Then holding up the calendar which was in front of her on the desk, Kitty said "Well good for you Vanessa. Sorry that I have to change the subject, but you are completely booked for today starting at noon".

Then with a little giggle, she said "All regular clients of yours who obviously couldn't wait to get back here and get their ass whipped after spending the long holiday season with their spouses!"

I laughed and as I headed down to the Mistress lounge to get ready for my busy day, I stopped, and turned back to Kitty and said "I was wondering if you would have a problem if some night after I got off of work, I brought Rick up here so that I could use one of the dungeons and really give him a taste of what Female Domination is all about".

"I have absolutely no problem with that at all Vanessa since Rick is not one of our clients and you do such a wonderful job for me. Just let me know when you are going to do that and which room you want to use"

I threw her a kiss and said, "Thanks Kitty". Then I hurried down to the lounge to get ready for my first appointment.

Not only was I kept busy my entire shift on Tuesday dominating regular clients of mine, but I also never got a chance to take a break on Wednesday or Thursday because of all the new clients who came in after having seen our internet ads and then deciding to select me as the Mistress they wanted for their session.

Since a significant portion of the population in the country had started using the internet during the preceding year, the website and the ads which Kitty had set up really started to pay off, and as we got more and more new customers from the website, she moved most of her advertising money from newspaper advertising over to advertising on the internet.

By the time that I finished up at 5 pm on Thursday after seeing my last client, to whom I had given a severe whipping, my thong was absolutely drenched from my arousal, and I knew that I was in serious need of a sexual release.

After clearing it with Kitty and making arrangements to use one of the dungeon rooms, I picked up the phone and called Rick's office. He answered the phone promptly and said "Good afternoon. This is Rick. How may I help you?"

I am sure that I caught him totally off guard when I said "Slave, This is Mistress Vanessa. Do you still have the business card with my address on it?"

After a slight hesitation, he regrouped and said "Oh yes. Of course, I do Mistress. I have it in my wallet".

"Very good. I'll expect you to be here at my place of business at 6 pm, and slave don't be late, or you'll regret it!"

Rather than change, I decided to meet Rick wearing the same outfit which I had just worn during the session with my last client. So, clad in a black leather bustier, black leather garter belt, a miniscule black leather thong, and thigh high black leather boots with four inch stiletto heels, I collected the items which I knew that I would need for when Rick arrived. I then went down to the Medieval Dungeon and prepared everything for his arrival.

At 6:15 pm, the door to the Dungeon opened, and Kitty said, "Mistress Vanessa, you have a visitor here who I believe you were expecting".

She ushered Rick into the dungeon and then closed the door behind her.

I could immediately see that Rick's eyes were as big as saucers as he quickly gazed around the Medieval Dungeon, looking at all the bondage equipment and implements of torture.

As I sat there on the red velvet seat of the ornate throne in the dungeon, with a grave look on my face, I said "Slave, get completely undressed and get down on your knees right now!"

From my demeanor and the tone of my voice, Rick could tell that I was not in the mood for any conversation at all, so he quickly removed his suit jacket, shirt, pants, underwear, shoes and socks. Then naked, he dropped down to the floor on his knees.

"Very good slave. Now crawl over here to me and kneel in front of my throne!"

As soon as Rick had complied with my order, I said "Since you agreed the other night to be my slave, I am going to formally start your training today so that you know exactly how I expect you to serve me and exactly what I expect from you".

I then pushed his head down to the top of my thigh high boots and said "The first rule which you will always remember slave is that whenever you come into my presence you will drop down onto your knees immediately and kiss and worship my high heel shoes or boots to signify that you are subservient to my wishes. Can you remember that rule slave?"

Rick quickly nodded his head and said, "Yes Mistress". Then he brought his mouth down to my boots and began kissing and licking them. I smiled to myself as I watched him lick and kiss every inch of both of my thigh high boots, and I happily reflected on the fact that I really did enjoy having a male, other than the clients who paid for domination, who was totally submissive to me.

When I was totally satisfied with the job that Rick had done on my boots, I said "Very good slave. That is the type of adoration which I will expect from you every time that you see me! Do you understand slave?"

Without so much as raising his head up, Rick said "Yes Mistress Vanessa".

I then stood up from my throne, walked over to the control panel on the wall, and lowered the suspension device which hung from the ceiling over the middle of the dungeon. I then looked at Rick and said, "Crawl over here slave and kneel in front of me".

As soon as Rick had followed my instructions, I grabbed his right wrist, lifted it up to one of the shackles attached to the suspension bar, and secured his wrist into the shackle. Then without wasting any time at all, I grabbed his left wrist, and secured it into the other shackle which was attached to the bar on the suspension device. Then I said to Rick "You may go ahead and stand up now slave!"

As soon as Rick was on his feet, I went over to the control panel on the wall and pressed the button which began raising the suspension device. I kept raising the bar connected to the suspension device until Rick's arms were pulled up high and taut above his head, and he was forced to stand on the tips of his toes to maintain his balance.

I patted Rick on his ass, and asked "Are you feeling helpless slave?"

"Yes Mistress. Quite helpless".

"Good. That's the way that I like my slaves".

I then went over to the rack on the wall which held all the implements of punishment, selected my favorite Cat-Of-Nine Tails Whip, and then stood behind Rick and said "The first thing which I need to do before we go any further with your training is to punish you for arriving late. You violated my rule which says that a slave will always be punctual when summoned by the Mistress. I told you to be here no later than 6 pm and in spite of my order, you showed up at 6:15 pm. Did you not slave?"

Rick immediately began to defend himself by saying "I am so sorry Mistress that I was late, but as soon as I got off of the phone with you, one of my clients called to ask me some questions and to put in a stock trade. I did the best that I could do to hurry up and finish the phone call with the client and then grab a cab to get over here".

I ran the tip of the whip down Rick's spine, and said "Well obviously slave, your best was not good enough since you were late, and you made me sit here waiting for you. Therefore, since you were 15 minutes late, you will receive 15 lashes from my whip as your punishment!"

Before Rick could even say anything, I stepped back and brought my whip down hard across his shoulder blades. He immediately let out a scream, but before his body had totally processed the pain from the first strike of the whip, I brought it back down once again even harder across the cheeks of his ass.

I then began alternating the strikes from my Cat-Of-Nine Tails whip between Rick's ass and his back until I had delivered all of the fifteen strokes which I had promised to him. By the time that I had finished, Rick was sobbing, and tears were running down his face. I was impressed however that he never uttered his safe word but that he took all of the punishment which I administered to him. I then stood back and admired the neat rows of red marks which I had left on Rick's back and ass, and said "Hopefully, you'll make sure that you are not late again when I summon you slave!"

I then moved in front of Rick, and I quickly noticed that his cock was pointing out straight in front of him hard and erect. I ran my hand over the shaft of his cock and said "Well slave, from all the crying which you were just doing, I thought that you didn't like that whipping, but your hard cock is telling me something else. You obviously enjoyed being whipped by me, didn't you slave?"

As he began to compose himself, Rick said "Yes Mistress. Thank you, Mistress. I am sorry that I disappointed you by being late".

I smiled and said "You are quite welcomed slave. Just remember what I said. Don't you dare be late the next time that I call you or I can assure you that you won't be thanking me by the time that I am done punishing you!"

At that point, I went over to the control panel on the wall, and lowered the suspension device, and at the same time ordered Rick to get down on his knees. I grabbed a pair of handcuffs out of the cabinet, and as soon as I had released Rick's wrists from the shackles, I pulled his arms behind his back, and locked his wrists together with the handcuffs.

I picked up a riding crop, smacked Rick on the ass, and ordered him to crawl over to the metal cage which was against the wall. As soon as he crawled over to the cage, I opened the door, guided him into it with the tip of my boot, and then locked the door of the cage. Since the cage was only about three feet high and five feet long, Rick was forced to remain on his knees with his arms handcuffed behind his back.

"Are you feeling totally helpless slave?"

Rick nodded his head and in a very docile tone of voice said, "Yes Mistress".

"Good! That's the way you should feel. Do you realize slave that I could go home now and leave you locked up in that cage until I come to work tomorrow, and that there is absolutely nothing that you can do if I should decide to leave you locked in that cage overnight?"

With a look of fear manifested all over his face, and in a sincere and pleading manner, Rick said "Please Mistress Vanessa. I beg you not to do that. Please don't leave me like this all night. I promise that I will do anything that you want me to do".

I smiled to myself because that was exactly what I had hoped that Rick would say. In his helpless condition, he obviously was now primed and ready to seriously consider the demands which I was about to present to him.

I went over to the ornate throne, sat down, crossed my legs, and said "Well slave, if you don't want to spend the night locked up like that in the cage, then I would suggest that you pay serious attention to what I am going to say to you".

"Yes Mistress. Whatever you say".

I smiled to myself, and then said "Slave, I assume that you do not work on Saturday and Sunday. Is that correct?"

Rick nodded and said "Yes Mistress. I only work Monday through Friday. The brokerage house is closed on the weekends".

"Good, that's what I thought. Well, you should not make any week end plans from this point forward. I will expect you to be available 24/7 for me on Saturdays and Sundays. Since you are now my slave, I will expect you to be free on those days for cleaning my apartment, doing my laundry, taking care of the food shopping, running errands as needed, and of course servicing me in any manner which I should desire. I might also decide to have you serve my roommates at some time in the future. Do you understand what I am saying slave?"

I could tell that Rick was somewhat shocked by what I had just said, but after a minute of reflection, he humbly said "Yes Mistress Vanessa. I understand what you are telling me".

"Very good slave. Since I like to sleep in a little later on the weekends when I don't have to go to work, I will expect you to report to my apartment on Saturday at 10 am sharp. Do you understand that slave?"

Obviously already showing the signs of discomfort from being incarcerated in the small cage, Rick said "Yes Mistress. I understand what you are telling me. I will be at your apartment on Saturday at 10am".

"Great. Now that we have that out of the way, I need you to pay attention carefully to what I am going to tell you now".

I then held up the large Stainless Steel Chastity Tube which I had previously taken from the cabinet in the Sissy Maid Room, and said "Slave, do you know what this is?"

With an absolute look of horror on his face, Rick said "Mistress, I have never seen one of those before in real life, but I have seen them on Internet websites which I have visited".

"Good slave. Then you are aware that this is a Male Chastity Tube".

Then with a big smile on my face, I said "Slave, I am not particularly worried about you having sex behind my back, but I am definitely concerned about you masturbating behind my back. I need to make sure that from this point forward you are never able to enjoy an orgasm unless I give you permission to have one. Therefore, before you leave here tonight, I am going to lock up that cock of yours in this nice stainless steel cage, so that I don't have to worry at all about you masturbating when you are not with me".

Then with a big smile, I said "Slave, since you are so well endowed this cage might be a little tight on you, even though it is the largest size which they make. However, it should serve its purpose just fine, and prevent you from having any type of an erection. I will hold the key to this device, and from now on, I will control your orgasms!"

Rick started shaking his head and said "Please Mistress. Don't lock me up in that thing. I promise you that I won't masturbate without your permission. There's no need to lock me up in that cage".

I laughed, and said "Rick, that sounds good, but you are a highly sexed male, and I am quite aware of what men do when they are sexually excited. No, I am sorry. If you want to be my slave and serve me, then that cock of yours will be locked in this chastity tube. I will hold the key and I will control your orgasms. I'm sorry but the chastity cage is not a negotiable part of our new relationship!"

I then began straightening up the dungeon and putting everything away while leaving Rick locked in the cage. When I was finished, I said "Slave, I am going to go down to the lounge and get changed out of these clothes before I go home. When I come back, you will either agree to have this chastity tube locked on your cock and balls, or I will just leave you in that cage until I come back to work tomorrow. It's your choice!"

I left the dungeon, went down to the Mistress lounge, and removed my work outfit. I freshened up in the Mistresses' restroom, and then got dressed in a sheer blouse, black leather slacks and my black patent pumps.

When I returned to the dungeon, opened the door, and entered, I could see that Rick had his head down on the floor of the cage, and appeared to be whimpering.

I walked over and stood in front of the cage, and said "What's the matter slave? Are you in pain?"

When Rick lifted his head up and looked at me, he shook his head, and said "No Mistress. I am not in pain. I am just very uncomfortable. Every part of my body is aching from being bent over like this. Could you please unlock this cage and let me out?"

"That depends on whether or not you have decided to comply with my wishes. Have you?"

After a long hesitation, Rick sighed, and said "Yes Mistress. I will comply with your wishes and let you lock me up in that chastity tube".

I shook my head, and said "Slave, that didn't sound very submissive or very sincere. You need to do much better than that. Since you made me wait for an answer, I think that you should now beg me properly and ask me to lock up that cock of yours in my chastity tube!"

Almost on the verge of crying, Rick said "Please Mistress Vanessa. I beg you to lock up my cock in your chastity tube. I beg you to please be my Key Holder and control all of my orgasms from this day forward".

With a big smile, I said "Well slave, since you asked me so nicely, I will be glad to lock up that cock of yours and take control of the key to your chastity tube!"

I then unlocked the padlock on the cage, opened the door, and allowed Rick to back out of the cage on his knees. I then helped him up onto his feet since he was a little shaky after having been kneeling in the cage for so long. I held onto his arm until he had properly established his balance, and then I led him over to the table next to my throne.

I picked up the stainless steel chastity tube and said "Slave, I am so glad that you truly want to serve me and to please me. Let's get this cock of yours locked up and then you can take me out to dinner and we can talk some more about what I expect out of our new relationship".

I tried on two different sizes of the hinged rings before I found the one which fit nice and snug around Rick's balls. I slid the stainless cage down over his cock, slid the rivet through the ring and the back of the cage, and locked everything together with one of my brass padlocks. Even though Rick's large cock was totally flaccid, there was no room at all in the cage for him to have an erection, just as I correctly had assumed would be the case.

I smiled, held the two keys for the padlock up in front of Rick's face, and then I slipped the keys down into my bra, and said "When I get home, I'll put one of these keys on a necklace and I'll put the other key away for safe keeping. Whenever you see the key that I wear on my necklace, it will be a constant reminder to you that you are no longer in control of your manhood, and that you are totally dependent on me for any future orgasms".

I then unlocked the handcuffs, freeing Rick's wrists and allowed him to get dressed and freshen up before heading down to the lobby with him.

When we walked into the lobby, Kitty was just getting ready to leave for the day. She turned to me and said "Well Vanessa. Did you and your new slave have a nice time?"

With a big smile, I said "I absolutely did Kitty. So much so that I'll need to pay you tomorrow for a stainless steel Chastity Tube which I am taking home with me and will not be returning to you!"

The Benefits Of Having A Personal Slave

During the year after I locked Rick up in his chastity tube, everything in both my personal life and my career were as close to perfect as anyone could ever hope for.

My clientele base increased dramatically because of the Internet advertising which Kitty was doing, and from all the referrals which my existing clients made on behalf of me.

By the fall of 2000, I was bringing home just about $2,500 every week. Kitty was almost as ecstatic as me about how well I was doing, and she was not shy when it came to letting all the other Mistresses know that I, after being there only two years had become the number three income producer at The House of Female Domination, right behind Alicia and Joan.

On the home front, things were also wonderful for me. With the exception of a few weekends when Rick had to go out of town on business, he showed up at my door every Saturday morning promptly at 10am.

As soon as he arrived, I would hand him a shopping list and money and send him back out to do the weekly food shopping for me and my roommates. When he returned with all of the items which were on my shopping list, he was then required to put everything away in the proper place.

Once that was done, Rick was required to remove all of his clothes, and then naked except for his chastity tube, he would begin vacuuming the carpets, dusting all the furniture, scrubbing the kitchen and bathroom, and cleaning our apartment from top to bottom.

Either I or Alicia or Joan, would inspect every cleaning task which Rick performed, and whenever one of us found that he did not properly complete every task which was assigned to him, or that we were not one hundred percent satisfied with the job that he had done, then he would be punished.

Usually not a weekend went by that Rick did not find himself bent over the couch in the living room where he would receive a whipping or paddling from either me or one of my roommates for failing to meet our stringent performance standards.

In all honesty, I would have to say that Rick actually did a wonderful job on the cleaning tasks and chores which were assigned to him. However, I fully understood that it is important that a Mistress insist on absolute perfection from her slave at all times when grooming him to serve her properly, and to never accept performance from a slave which is less than one hundred percent perfection.

As I mentioned earlier, Rick was always kept naked when performing his chores around our apartment. The only time that I ever allowed Rick to wear any clothes was when he had to go down to the basement laundry to wash and dry our clothes and bedding. In addition to doing the general laundry, he was always required to hand wash all of my lingerie in the sink, according to the specific instructions which I had given to him, and to hang all of my delicate underwear up in the bathroom to air dry.

The highlight of each weekend for me, of course, was when Rick was finished with all of his chores, and I would then use him for my sexual pleasure. Most weekends I would lock his wrists behind his back with handcuffs, and then as I would sit on the chair in my bedroom, I would have him use his mouth and tongue for hours, giving me all of the orgasms which I desired, until my needs were totally satiated. Then, in spite of his inevitable begging for a release, I would send him home totally frustrated and horny.

Usually once a month however, as a reward for his servitude to me, I would restrain Rick down helplessly to my bed, keep him overnight, remove his chastity tube, and use his glorious cock time and time again for my pleasure. Then at whatever time we woke up the next morning, I would usually make him take me out to breakfast or brunch.

Many weekends, after watching Rick prance around my apartment completely naked all day performing his chores, I was tempted to unlock his chastity tube, and use his cock instead of his mouth and tongue for my pleasure.

I avoided doing that however because I preferred to keep him as horny as possible most of the time, so that he would always be subservient to my wishes and do whatever I ordered him to do, in the hope that I might unlock his chastity tube and give him a release if I was pleased with his service.

One weekend after Rick had left our apartment after completing all of his chores and pleasuring me with his mouth and tongue, I was relaxing in the living room with Alicia and Joan chatting and enjoying a glass of wine, when Alicia said "Vanessa, Rick has been serving you as your slave for almost nine months now, and both Joan and I think that you have done a great job training him".

"Well, thank you Alicia. I appreciate that".

Then after a slight hesitation, she said "However, there was something which I wanted to discuss with you. Joan and I were talking about Rick the other day, and we thought that it might be time for you to take him to the next level of servitude".

I looked at Alicia with a quizzical look on my face, shook my head, and said "I am not sure that I know exactly what you mean when you say next level of servitude".

Alicia nodded, and said "Ok Vanessa, here's what we were thinking. As we all know, Rick would be considered a real prize by most women. He is a very intelligent, successful, handsome and well-endowed male".

I looked at her, smiled, and said "Yes. I would agree with you on that".

"Well, we were thinking that the only time that Rick really experiences your domination is on the weekends when you have him here doing chores around our apartment. Correct?"

"Well no. That's not exactly true Alicia. Rick experiences my domination and control 24/7 because he is locked up in that chastity tube and he knows that only I have the key which can give him a release"

"Ok, I won't argue with you on that point because you are right that the chastity tube is the primary means by which you control Rick. We were just thinking that after having him as a slave for so many months, that maybe you should push him a little deeper into submission and servitude to you and take some steps to break down his male ego and emasculate him further".

I took a long sip of my wine, and then asked, "Exactly what did you have in mind Alicia?"

"Well Vanessa, we were thinking that some feminization and sissy maid training for Rick would probably be appropriate at this time. It would help to completely dispel any vestiges of his alpha male ego which are still left. You could make him start wearing panties or panty hose to work every day and make him start dressing up as a sissy maid while he does the chores around our apartment. Joan and I would love to help you convert him into a real sissy maid. Gosh, we could even invite some of our girl friends over for a party and we could use your sissy maid to wait on them and entertain them".

I sat there quietly for a few minutes thinking about what Alicia had just said and I realized that I really did like the idea of feminizing Rick and using him as a sissy maid. My mind started wandering and before I knew it, I was thinking of a multitude of ways that I could humiliate him, use him, and have lots of fun at his expense.

When I finally spoke, I said "Ok Alicia. I like the idea. How do you propose that we proceed?"

With a big smile, Alicia said "Awesome Vanessa. Why don't we do this? When Rick shows up this coming Saturday morning, instead of having him do chores around the apartment, let's take him shopping for lingerie, outfits, and shoes. I'll go with you and by the time that we are done, Rick, or maybe we should more appropriately call him

Rikki, will have a nice assortment of lingerie and sissy outfits to wear. What do you think?"

I smiled, got up from the couch, gave Alicia a big high five, and said "Ok girl. That sounds like a plan. I better call Rick and tell him to make sure that he has his credit cards with him when he comes over here on Saturday".

Alicia laughed, and said "Yes Vanessa, I have a feeling that by the time that you and I are done picking out clothes for Rick, we will make a big dent in his credit cards!"

Shopping For My Sissy Slave

On Friday afternoon as I was leaving work, and while he was still at the office, I left a message on Rick's home answering machine. All I said was "Slave, this is Mistress Vanessa. When you come over to my apartment tomorrow morning, make sure that you bring your credit cards with you. We will be doing a little bit of shopping on Saturday and you need to be prepared to pay for the items which we will purchase. Hugs. See you tomorrow!"

On Saturday morning after I took my shower, I got dressed in an outfit which I knew would definitely catch Rick's attention. I put on a new black leather tank top which I had recently purchased from Neiman Marcus and a pair of skin tight black leather jeans, as well as my black leather pumps with four inch heels.

When the intercom rang promptly at 10 am, I buzzed Rick into the building, opened the door of the apartment, and then waited for him to come up to the second floor. As soon as he came up to the second floor landing and saw me, he said "Wow Mistress. You look awesome!"

"Well, thank you very much slave. I am glad that you like my outfit".

Then gesturing to the open door, I said "Come on in. We're just waiting for Alicia to finish getting dressed and then we'll go".

With a confused look on his face, Rick said "Oh, is your roommate going shopping with us this morning?"

As I closed the door behind us, I said "Yes, Alicia is good friends with the owners of a couple of shops which specialize in the things that we need to buy today, so she was kind enough to offer to take us around today".

"Oh, that's nice Mistress. I brought my credit cards like your message told me to do. What do we need to get for you today?"

I laughed, and said "Slave, we don't need to get anything for me today. We are actually going shopping for you. There's quite a few things which we need to purchase for you!"

It was obvious that Rick was totally puzzled by my answer, but before he had a chance to ask me any more questions, Alicia came walking out of her bedroom, and Rick's eyes were immediately transfixed on the outfit which she was wearing.

Alicia was wearing her favorite black leather bustier, which was quite revealing, and a short black leather jacket over the bustier. Her black leather mini-skirt was so short that it only came down to the middle of her thighs and helped accentuate her long legs which were encased in black fishnet hose. Her black leather knee high boots had stiletto heels that were at least four inches high and embellished her already stunning figure.

As soon as she walked into the living room, Alicia went over to Rick, kissed him on the cheek, and said "So nice to see you again slave. I am sure that Mistress Vanessa has told you that we are going to take you shopping today. I am so looking forward to it. It should be quite a fun experience. Well, at least for Mistress Vanessa and I!"

Rick didn't say a word, but I smiled to myself. Knowing Alicia, I knew that she would probably humiliate Rick to no end before the day was over.

As I grabbed my coat, and we headed down the stairs to hail a cab, Alicia said "Slave, since we are so nice and have agreed to take you shopping today, you obviously will not be able to clean the apartment and do your chores like you normally do on Saturdays. I'll assume that you will notify Mistress Vanessa as to which night this week you will plan on coming over to take care of all your chores!"

As we got into the cab in front of our apartment building, Alicia smiled and said "We have two stops to make today, but they are both close together in the Chelsea Area. I've already made the phone calls and set everything up, so my friends will be expecting us".

Alicia gave an address on West 28th Street to the cab driver, and then turned to me and said "You'll love this store. They've been around forever, and we should be able to get everything that we need for your slave in one place"

After Alicia's comment, I wondered to myself why we were going to be making two stops today, if she felt that we could buy all the lingerie and outfits which we needed for Rick at the first store. I decided not to pose my question to her, and just go along for the fun, and see what Alicia had planned.

When the cab pulled up in front of our first destination, I saw that the Fetish Clothing & Lingerie Shop, which was located on the second floor of a five store building, had a huge display window which featured many of their sexy outfits.

After Rick paid the cab driver and we all stepped out onto the sidewalk in front of the store, he took a good look at all of the sexy lingerie displayed in the front window of the store. He then turned to me, and said "Mistress, you said earlier that we would be shopping for me today and not you. Is that still the case?"

With a big smile on my face, I said "Yes slave. That is definitely the case. We are here to buy some lingerie and outfits specifically for you, and I will expect you to fully cooperate with us and any salespeople you meet. If I should hear any arguments out of you today or feel that you are being disrespectful at all, then I will punish you like you've never been punished before. Do you understand what I am saying slave?"

Rick hesitated answering me for a minute, and then with a worrisome look on his face, said "Yes Mistress. I understand what you are saying".

As soon as we entered the store, a tall very attractive redhead who was probably in her late twenties or early thirties came rushing over to Alicia, gave her a hug, kissed her on the cheek, and then said "Alicia, wow you look amazing. Do you realize that you haven't been in here to see me for almost a year?"

Alicia sighed, and gave the woman another big hug, and said "I know. You are right. I am so sorry. We need to get together, and have you come over some night to our apartment and play with Joan and me".

That comment brought a big smile to the woman's face, and she said "Well, I will definitely take you up on that offer!"

Alicia then turned to me, and said "Vanessa, this is my good friend Lorraine, and she has agreed to help us get everything that we need today".

Lorraine quickly gave me a hug and said "It is so nice to meet you Vanessa. Alicia has already told me what a wonderful roommate and coworker you are. She just didn't tell me how gorgeous you are!"

"Well Lorraine, I appreciate that nice comment, especially coming from someone as attractive as yourself!"

Then as if she noticed Rick for the first time, Lorraine said "Vanessa, is this the slave who Alicia told me about when she called me?"

"Yes Lorraine. This is my slave Rick, and hopefully we will be able to get all the lingerie, outfits, shoes, and accessories which we need for him".

"Oh, absolutely Vanessa. Well, I'll get started with him and pick out his lingerie first. Is there anything in particular that you would like to see your slave wear?"

I explained to Lorraine that I wanted Rick to have at least a dozen pairs of sexy panties so that I could have him wear a pair to work each day under his clothing. I also told her that he needed to have a couple of bras with built in falsies so that when he wore outer female garments they would fit him properly. In addition to those items, I wanted him to have a garter belt, a good selection of stockings, some pantyhose, and a nice satin boned corset.

"No problem at all Vanessa. Why don't you and Alicia sit down and relax while I take your slave and put together a selection of items which I think will please you".

While Alicia and I sat down and chatted, Lorraine took out a cloth measuring tape, wrote down all of Rick's measurements, and then began guiding him around the store, picking out different pieces of underwear.

As soon as Rick was out of earshot, Alicia filled me in on where we would be going when we were finished buying clothes and shoes for Rick. She felt that I should know what was involved at our next stop so that I was prepared to handle my slave in case he put up any resistance.

About a half hour later, with her arms full of merchandise, Lorraine returned, placed everything down on the table next to me, and said "Ok Vanessa. I believe that we've got everything that you mentioned plus a few extra things which I think that you will like. All of these items should fit your slave perfectly, so I'll just leave everything here for you and Alicia to look at. If there's anything that you don't like, please let me know. Now what did you have in mind for your slave as far as outer garments are concerned?"

I told Lorraine that I definitely wanted Rick to have a French Maid's Outfit and a pair of black high heel pumps which he could wear when my roommates and I made him serve our guests at parties which took place at our apartment. I also wanted him to have a glitzy red dress and a pair of open toe red high heels in case I decided to really humiliate him by taking him out on the town some evening.

Lorraine laughed, and said "I am so glad that you know exactly what you want for your slave. It makes my job so much easier".

As she started to walk away, I said "Oh Lorraine, I noticed that you have a very nice selection of wigs. I think that I'd like to see my slave as a blonde with long hair when I dress him up"

"No problem at all Vanessa. I'll pick out a very nice blonde wig for him".

Then turning to Rick, she said "Ok slave, let's go get you fitted for those outfits, shoes, and wig which your Mistress wants!"

About twenty five minutes later, Lorraine returned with the outfits, wig, and shoes, and said "Well, we did it. I think that you will be pleased with the things that I selected for your slave".

After looking at all of the lingerie, the elegant satin corset, the French Maid's outfit, the sexy cocktail dress, the beautiful blonde wig, and the high heel shoes which Lorraine had selected for Rick, I said "Lorraine, you did an absolutely wonderful job. I love everything that you picked out for my slave, and I can't wait to see him model it all for me!"

Once Lorraine had packaged up all the clothing and shoes into two shopping bags, she presented Rick with a bill which was over $1,400 and I wondered if he would raise an objection. Instead, he quietly handed her his credit card, signed the voucher, and took the bags which contained his new female attire.

After Lorraine promised to come over to our apartment and see us some time, she once again gave Alicia and me a hug before we left the store. As soon as we stepped out onto the sidewalk, Alicia said "We can just walk over to our next appointment since it is right on West 27th Street and they will be expecting us in about fifteen minutes".

As we crossed Sixth Avenue and headed to our destination, I smiled to myself knowing that Rick was not going to be pleased at all once he found out what we had planned for him. I on the other hand, was rather thrilled about the idea, and I couldn't wait to see how Rick would look when they were finished working on him.

Ten minutes later, we arrived at our destination which was on the second floor of a four story office building, and as soon as we reached the second floor landing, and Rick saw the sign on the door which read "Hair Removal Studio", he turned to me and with his voice quivering said "Oh no Mistress Vanessa. You don't really expect me to go in here and have all of my hair removed. Do you?"

I laughed and said "Of course not slave. No one is going to touch any of that beautiful hair on your head. We just need to have all the hair that's everywhere else on your body removed by waxing!"

Rick started shaking his head and said, "Why Mistress? No, I don't like this idea at all. I've heard that it really hurts having your hair removed like that"

At that point with a frown on her face, Alicia interjected herself into the conversation and said "Slave, you listen to me right now. Your Mistress wants you to look attractive in all those pretty new clothes which you just bought, and there's no way that you will look pretty in that beautiful lingerie with all that ugly hair on your body. Now, open that door and get your butt inside right now!"

I held my breath for a moment and wondered if Rick would utter his safe word and refuse to go into the salon. A second later however, he opened the door and walked into the waiting area of the salon with Alicia and I right behind him.

When the door was opened, a bell rang, alerting the business that someone had come in. A few seconds later, an amiable man who I judged to be in his forties came bouncing into the lobby. He was wearing a red satin shirt which was open almost all the way down to his navel, and multiple gold chains hung around his neck.

As soon as he saw Alicia, he ran over to her, kissed her on both cheeks, held his arms up in the air, clapped his hands, and said "Oh Alicia, I am so glad to see you again Sweetie. It's been a while since you brought me any business".

Alicia smiled, and said "Well Marcus, that's because I haven't run across any slaves till today who were in need of your service".

Marcus then looked at me, and said "Alicia, you didn't tell me that another beautiful sexy woman besides you was coming to see me today".

Alicia laughed, and said "Marcus, this is my roommate Mistress Vanessa. The slave that you are working on today actually belongs to her".

"Oh my, two gorgeous Mistresses grace my doorstep at the same time. I don't know if I can handle this. I might just have to go straight for a while".

Alicia snickered, and said "No, I don't think that will ever happen Marcus. That would upset too many of your lovers!"

With a big smile on his face, Marcus said "Yes, my dear, I suppose that you are right. So, I assume that this good looking guy with you is our client today?"

I patted Rick on his back and said "Yes Marcus. This is my slave Rick".

Marcus nodded, and said "I understand from Alicia that we are doing a full body waxing from the neck to the toes. Is that right?"

I smiled, and said "Yes Marcus, that is correct. I want all the hair removed from his neck down to his toes".

"Great, well let's take him into the back and we'll have him get completely undressed".

Marcus led us down the hallway adjoining the lobby and into the customer lounge which had a couch, restroom, beverages, and lockers for the clients' belongings and said, "Ok ladies, go ahead and get your slave naked and I'll notify Patrick who is our best cosmetologist to go ahead and get a room ready for him".

As he started to walk out of the lounge, Marcus stopped, slapped the side of his face, and said "Oh my, I almost forgot. Alicia mentioned on the phone earlier that your slave is wearing a chastity tube. We will need that removed so that we can do a complete job on his cock and balls. Do you have the key with you?"

I lifted the key up which was attached to my necklace and said "No problem at all Marcus. I'll remove his chastity cage".

Marcus blew me a kiss and said "Great. Thank you so much. I'll go ahead and make sure that Patrick has everything ready since I plan on assisting him today".

As soon as Rick was completely naked, I reached into my purse, retrieved a pair of handcuffs, and told him to place his arms behind his back.

Somewhat agitated by the situation, Rick said "Mistress, is that really necessary. Do you have to handcuff me in front of these gay men?"

I smiled to myself, knowing that the humiliation that Rick was going to be subjected to would almost be as bad as the waxing.

With an unsympathetic look on my face, I said "Yes slave. It is definitely necessary because we need to remove this chastity tube so that they can do a proper waxing job on you, and I am not removing that cage until your wrists are restrained behind your back!"

Realizing that there was no way that I was going to back down, Rick placed his arms behind his back, and I locked his wrists together with the handcuffs. I then used the key which was on my necklace to unlock the padlock on the chastity tube, freed Rick's cock, and then put his chastity cage in my purse.

You never would have suspected that he was scared to death about the waxing which he would soon endure, because as soon as I removed the chastity tube, Rick's cock sprung up out in front of him hard and erect.

About five minutes later, Marcus returned to the lounge, and the minute he saw Rick standing there handcuffed with a raging hard-on, he put his hand on his right cheek, giggled, and said "Oh my goodness. Look at that beautiful piece of manhood. I would say that someone is very excited about having the hair ripped off his cock and balls today!"

When Marcus made that graphic comment, it dawned on me that the pain which Rick was probably going to experience during the waxing of his genitals would most likely be worst than any of the cock and ball torture that I had inflicted on him so far, and I hoped that he would be able to cope with it.

Marcus told us that it would probably be about two hours before they were finished with Rick since they were doing a total body procedure, so as Marcus led Rick down to the waxing room, Alicia and I decided to leave the studio and go have lunch.

Alicia and I walked the short distance back over to Sixth Avenue where we found a delightful Korean restaurant. We both ordered the lunch special which consisted of BBQ Chicken Chulpan and Miso Soup, as well as a bottle of Chardonnay.

As we sat there enjoying our wine, I reached out, touched Alicia's hand and said "Alicia, I really want to thank you for making the arrangements and setting everything up today for my slave. I am so glad that you convinced me to take the steps necessary to turn Rick into a sissy slave".

"It was my pleasure Vanessa. I can't wait to see how your slave looks once we do his make-up and get him into his new wig, lingerie, and heels. If he looks really good as a sissy, Joan and I might even have to borrow him from you some night and have some fun using him".

I laughed and said "I have no problem with that at all. You just let me know when you want him!"

After a long leisurely lunch, Alicia and I headed back over to the studio, and were greeted by Marcus as soon as we walked in.

With his very animated mannerisms, he said "Hello Ladies, did you have a nice lunch?"

I smiled and said "Yes Marcus. We had a delicious meal at a lovely Korean restaurant. So, how are things coming along with my slave?"

"Oh, that beautiful specimen of a slave is all done, and his hairless body is all smooth and shiny, and oh so gorgeous. He's sitting in the customer lounge waiting for you, since he couldn't really go anywhere with those handcuffs on his wrists".

Then with a little chuckle, Marcus said "Mistress, I think that your slave has probably stopped sobbing by now".

When Alicia and I entered the customer lounge, I was glad to see that Rick was composed and quietly sitting on the couch waiting for me to return.

"So, how did it go slave? Was it as bad as you thought it would be?"

In slow measured sentences, Rick said "No Mistress. It was much worse than I expected. Having the hair waxed off my back, chest, arms and legs was somewhat painful. Having the hair removed from my genitals was excruciating torture. It felt like the skin was literally being pulled off my cock and balls".

I saw Alicia put her hand over her mouth so that Rick wouldn't see her laughing at the misery which he obviously suffered, and I said, "Well slave, let's see what kind of job they did on you".

Alicia and I both went over to Rick and we began running our hands all over his back, arms, chest and legs.

When I felt how silky smooth his skin was, I squealed with delight, and said "Slave, I absolutely love the glassy feel of your smooth skin. I am so glad that Alicia convince me to have this done. Your legs will look so much more attractive now when you put on your new black stockings and heels without all that ugly hair in the way".

Then Alicia slipped her hand between his legs and ran it all over Rick's cock and balls and said "Very nice! Everything down here is as smooth as a new baby. Slave, you should be quite thankful that you won't have to worry about hairs getting caught in your chastity tube any more".

I reached into my purse, pulled out Rick's chastity tube, and said "Speaking of that, let's get you locked back up into your chastity cage before Alicia gets you all aroused, then I can remove those handcuffs and you can get dressed".

After I had Rick stand up, I slipped the hinged ring around his balls, slid the cage down over his cock, and pushed the rivet through the ring and the back of the cage. Then I slipped the padlock through the hole in the rivet, and snapped the lock shut, hearing that wonderful clicking sound which indicated that my slave's cock was once again securely locked up and was only accessible to me.

I then unlocked the handcuffs, releasing Rick's wrists, and allowed him to get dressed. Once he was ready, we went back out to the lobby and with a big smile, Marcus said "So Mistress Vanessa, were you happy with the job that we did on your slave?"

"Marcus, you and Patrick did an absolutely wonderful job. I just love the way that my slave looks and feels without any hair on his body".

When Marcus totaled up the bill and presented it to Rick, I said "Slave, please make sure that you give Marcus an especially nice tip since he did such an awesome job getting all that hair off your body today!"

Once the bill was paid, Marcus looked at me and said "Mistress, I would suggest that you bring your slave in for another treatment in six weeks so that his hair doesn't start getting unruly again. Would you like me to make an appointment for you now?"

I could see that Rick didn't like that idea at all, but I smiled and said "Yes Marcus. Please go ahead and do that for me".

Marcus scheduled an appointment for Rick at the end of November and handed me the card. He then came around from behind the counter and gave me and Alicia a big hug and said, "Ladies, thanks so much for bringing your slave in today".

Then as we were getting ready to leave, Marcus with a very devilish grin said "Mistress Vanessa, if you should ever decide to expose your slave to some forced bi-action, please feel free to handcuff him and drop him off here. It's not everyday that Patrick and I see clients who are endowed so well as your slave".

Alicia and I laughed, and then, much to the chagrin of Rick, I said "Thanks Marcus. I will definitely keep your generous offer in mind!"

After we had made our way downstairs and out to the sidewalk to hail a cab, I turned to Rick and said "Slave, you can just bring all your new clothes and accessories over to our apartment now, and we'll plan on having you spend tonight with us. I can't wait to see how you will look after we do your make-up, paint your toenails, and get you all dressed up in your new wig and lingerie".

Then as the three of us were ready to get into a cab, I said "Slave, I was quite happy with the way that you accepted everything that we subjected you to today. I might even consider releasing you from that chastity tube and allowing you to have an orgasm tonight, as long as you properly pleasure me as my Sissy Slave!"

.... To Be Continued ....

Before You Go...

I hope that you enjoyed this book as much or more than <u>Part I</u> and <u>Part II</u> of this Series, and I sincerely thank you for reading my Novels. I realize that you have a tremendous choice of books to select from on Amazon, therefore I am honored that you decided to read my work.

I would really appreciate it if you would please take a few minutes to leave a Review for me on Amazon.

Not only am I interested in knowing what you thought about this novel, I also welcome any input you might wish to share with me, as I am currently working on Part IV of "What The Mistress Wants ...The Mistress Gets"

Also, don't forget to stop by my <u>Author's Page on Amazon</u>, and "Follow Me", so that you will be kept abreast of my activities and will be notified whenever I release a new Novel.

Thank you,

Mistress Vanessa

Made in the USA
San Bernardino, CA
31 May 2019